P9-DKF-791

ORCHARD BOOKS / NEW YORK

An Imprint of Scholastic Inc.

A Good Night Walk

ELISHA COOPER

Copyright

© 2005 by Elisha Cooper

All rights reserved. • Published by Orchard

Books, an imprint of Scholastic Inc. ORCHARD BOOKS and

design are registered trademarks of Watts Publishing Group, Ltd.,

used under license. SCHOLASTIC and associated logos are trademarks and/or

registered trademarks of Scholastic Inc. No part of this publication may be reproduced, stored in a

retrieval system, or transmitted in any form or by any means, electronic, mechanical,

photocopying, recording, or otherwise, without written permission of the

publisher. For information regarding permission, write to Orchard Books,

Scholastic Inc., Permissions Department, 557 Broadway, New York,

NY 10012.   Library of Congress Cataloging-in-Publication Data

Cooper, Elisha. A good night walk / by Elisha Cooper.—1st ed. p. cm.

Summary: The reader is taken on a journey through a neighborhood

and shown the sights, sounds, and smells as evening approaches.

ISBN 0-439-68783-7 • [1. Bedtime—Fiction. 2. Walking—Fiction.

3. Neighborhood—Fiction.] I. Title. PZ7.C784737Go 2005 [E]—dc22

10 9 8 7 6 5 4 3 2 1   05 06 07 08 09

Printed in Singapore   46 • First edition, September 2005

The text type was set in 21-point Cheltenham. • Watercolor and pencil were

used for the illustrations in this book. • Book design by Alison Klapthor

for zoë

Let's go for a walk, along the block,
and see what we can see, before it's time for bed.

The neighbor next door has finished her gardening.

She rests against the red wheelbarrow under the oak tree.

The leaves of the oak tree bend in the wind.

Its high branches bounce a pair of chattering squirrels.

The squirrels chase each other from the
telephone wire to the clothesline to the flag.

They race toward the bird feeder.

The birds circle the feeder, fluttering their wings.

The black-and-white cat goes to rest
in the shade of the apple tree.

The smell of apple pie pours out the kitchen window.

The screen door opens and shuts, echoing over the lawn.

The boys mow the lawn and
fill the trash cans with the cut grass.

The man from the post office delivers
the last mail of the day.

And there's the bay, with long boats on top,
and the round moon rising above.

Let's turn and walk back the way that we came.

The mail has been opened,

the trash cans brought to the curb.

The screen door is silent,

the apple pie eaten.

The black-and-white cat goes inside to sleep.

The birds are calm.

The flag is down, the clothes are in.

The telephone wires hum, the squirrels are quiet.

The oak tree is still.

The wind has settled.

The neighbor next door has put away

the red wheelbarrow and turned off the lights.

We're home. It's time for bed.
And all we have seen, we will see again,
when we walk along the block in the morning.